SHATTERED ILLUSIONS

SHATTERED ILLUSIONS

A JOURNEY FROM LOVE TO LIBERATION

ERICKA MOON

Ericka Moon

Shattered Illusions: A Journey from Love to Liberation

All rights reserved

Copyright © 2024 by Ericka Moon

Published by Publishing Platform

PREFACE

Sky's connection with God and her unshakable faith remain central to her journey. Her prayers were not born out of despair but out of a deep trust in God's plan. As she prayed for guidance, she drew strength from scriptures like Deuteronomy 31:6 and Isaiah 41:10, reminding her of God's constant presence and unwavering support. Sky's story is a powerful reminder that faith, independence, and resilience can carry us through even the most challenging times.

"In the darkest moments, we find our true strength."

Sky thought she had found the love of her life, but the man she trusted harbored dark secrets. In a world filled with abuse, lies, and shattered dreams, she embarks on a journey of survival, resilience, and ultimately, healing. Torn but Unbroken is not just a story-it's a testament to the human spirit's ability to rise above adversity. Discover the powerful journey of a woman who finds her strength, reclaims her life, and learns that true love begins with self-love.

This is a story for anyone who has ever felt broken, lost, or alone. Sky's journey will inspire you to find your own strength, break free from the chains of abuse, and embrace the peace and love you deserve. Her story is your story.

"Surviving isn't just about living through the storm- it's about learning to dance in the rain."

Turn the page and join Sky on a journey that will break your heart, then heal it. Torn but Unbroken will stay with you long after the last page is turned, reminding you that no matter how dark life gets, the light within you can never be extinguished.

Written with raw emotion and unflinching honesty, Torn but Unbroken is a reflection of Ericka Moon's personal journey through love, loss, and the ultimate triumph of the human spirit. Her story is a beacon of hope for anyone navigating the complexities of life and relationships.

What would you do if the love you thought would save you turned into the very thing that destroyed you? Torn but Unbroken is a gripping, heart-wrenching tale that explores the complexities of love, the pain of betrayal, and the incredible power of resilience.

FAITH & REVELATION: SKY'S JOURNEY WITH GOD

Sky's journey was marked by faith and trust in God. When overwhelmed by the brokenness of her relation- ship, she turned to prayer, asking God to open her eyes. God, in His infinite wisdom, revealed not only the truth of her own situation but also the struggles and deceptions in the lives of others, including her own family.

Sky clung to the promise in Deuteronomy 31: 6:

"Be strong and courageous. Do not be afraid or terrified because of them, for the Lord your God goes with you; He will never leave you nor forsake you."

This scripture became her anchor, reminding her that no matter how deep the darkness, God was with her, guiding her towards the light.

She found comfort in Isaiah 41: 10:

"So do not fear, for I am with you; do not be dismayed, for I am your God. I will strengthen you and help you; I will uphold you with my righteous right hand."

These verses grounded her in the understanding that her strength was not her own but rooted in her unwavering trust in God's plan.

Sky's story is a testament to the power of prayer and the importance of trusting in God's promises. Even in the most challenging situations, God's love and guidance are always available to those who seek Him.

CHAPTER 1: A CHANCE MEETING

In the heart-wrenching pages of this true story, we delve into the life of a woman who, with unwavering love and boundless patience, embarked on a journey with a man who had never known genuine love before her arrival. Little did she know that the love she so freely gave would lead her through the darkest and most tumultuous chapters of her life. The story begins with an unexpected phone call, a twist of fate that connects She and He. He had dialed the wrong number, and She happened to be on the other end. Their initial interaction is marked by surprise and curiosity.

A VOICE IN THE DARKNESS

As they converse over the phone, an undeniable connection begins to form. She's intrigued by the voice on the other end of the line, and he finds himself drawn to the warmth and kindness in her words. Despite their different backgrounds, they share a moment of genuine connection.

Their relationship progresses rapidly as they become entangled in the intensity of new found love. He initially appears to be a decent, respectful, kind, gentlemanly man. For a while, everything seems idyllic, and she envisions a future with him. However, the speed at which their love is developing blinds her to the impending challenges and the realization that she may be making the biggest mistake of her life. However, as things progress quickly, there are noticeable flaws that give her pause. She becomes wary of attachment and decides to go her way. Just when she thought she was walking away from what she perceived as a hasty love mistake, surprising Revelation shook her world. She discovers that she's pregnant, with his firstborn child. Her decision takes an unexpected turn as she shares the news with him, forever altering the course of their lives and leading them down a path filled with challenges and transformations.

CHAPTER 1.5: NAVIGATING PARENTHOOD

The arrival of their first child together marked a significant shift in their lives. For him in a world where the unlikeliest of love stories unfold, our tale begins with a woman who met and married the love of her life. He was a man who had never truly experienced a real relationship, nor had he ever felt the warmth of genuine love. But their paths crossed, and destiny wove them together in a way that neither could have foreseen. As their love story unfolded, she noticed small imperfections in him, quirks that she deemed endearing, yet not serious enough to deter her. With a heart full of hope and unwavering determination, she took it upon herself to give him the family life, and most importantly, the true love he had never known. Little did she know the storm that would soon brew within the man she loved.

CHAPTER 2

Secretly, he harbored a dark resentment, a hatred that he couldn't fully comprehend. He chose to stay, hard for him to let go; why? is the million dollar question, despite his hidden animosity, and as the years passed, his true nature began to surface. He used and abused her in ways she could never have imagined. The love that had once blossomed between them had withered, leaving behind only pain and despair. She had two children before they met and their family grew to include five more. But this love story was far from conventional, painted by heartbreak and tragedy. They even suffered the loss of one child due to the abusive turmoil that had become the norm.

CHAPTER 3

They spoke of growing old together and working through their issues, but he couldn't break free from his addictions. Love affairs and drug and alcohol abuse became his escape from the life they had built. He was never adept at hiding his transgressions; she always uncovered the truth. Despite his countless betrayals, she extended chance after chance hoping for redemption. Yet, the day came when she had given all she could, and she finally threw him to the wolves. In his descent, he landed right back where he had come from- a pit of despair.

CHAPTER 4

As the story unfolds, he bears the weight of guilt and remorse, trapped in his self-made hell. A man with a narcissistic personality must confront the consequences of his actions. "Torn but Unbroken" is a journey of love, heartbreak, and the resilience of the human spirit a story of healing and finding strength in the face of adversity.

CHAPTER 5

Amid the darkness that enveloped their lives, she found a glimmer of hope. The woman who had given her all to the man she loved emerged from the ashes, stronger and more determined than ever before. She faced the challenges that lay ahead with unwavering courage. With her children by her side and the memory of the child they had lost, she embarked on a journey of healing and self-discovery. The scars of her past served as a reminder of the strength that resided within her. She refused to be defined by the pain that had once consumed her.

CHAPTER 6

As she found her footing in the world without him, she also discovered that others had experienced similar hardships. In her quest for healing, she reached out to support groups and connected with those who understood the depths of her pain. The man who had torn their family apart remained entangled in the web of his own making. The weight of guilt and the consequences of his actions became inescapable. He found himself alone, abandoned by the very person who had tried so hard to help him.

CHAPTER 7

"Torn but Unbroken" is not just a story of heartbreak but a testament to the resilience of the human spirit. It's a journey of self-discovery, healing, and the power of love, both self-love and the love of those who stood by her. It's a reminder that no matter how broken we may become, there is always the potential for healing, growth, and the rekindling of a life worth living. In the end, the woman who had endured so much emerged from the storm, not as a victim but as a survivor. She found the strength to rebuild her life, to mend the wounds, and to teach her children that they, too, could rise above adversity.

CHAPTER 8

The world, with all its complexities, offered our protagonist a fresh canvas upon which to paint the story of her resurgence. As she ventured deeper into the realm of healing, her outreach to those who had endured similar hardships expanded. Her unwavering determination to break free from the past and construct a brighter future made her a beacon of hope to others. She dedicated herself to making a difference, volunteering and advocating for men and women, and sharing her experiences with those on the path to recovery. In their shared pain and triumph, they discovered the power of collective healing.

CHAPTER 9

Meanwhile, the man who had inflicted so much pain upon her remained mired in the consequences of his actions. Guilt, like an unshakable specter, haunted his every step. The life he had chosen was crumbling, and the solitude he had sought now seemed more desolate than ever. His soul ached with the knowledge of the love he had callously discarded, the unwavering devotion he had forsaken. He became an architect of his isolation, a man abandoned by the one who had, against all odds, tried to help him.

CHAPTER 10

Their father, who once stood at the center of our lives, had chosen a path of escape and self- destruction. His absence was felt deeply, not as a void but as a contrast to the nurturing environment we now embraced. He had abandoned his children, opting for a life that had dealt him nothing but hardship and disappointment. In his quest to escape responsibility, he had only succeeded in creating a larger chasm between himself and the family he once had.

He harbored resentment, not towards the circumstances that led to his downfall but towards me, for being the constant reminder of what he had lost. It was painful to witness his misplaced anger directed at the very children who bore no fault in his choices. His failure to support them, emotionally or financially, seemed like a futile attempt to beat a system designed to ensure his responsibilities were met.

Yet, no matter how much he tried to evade his obligations, the truth remained undeniable. Child support was a reality that would eventually catch up with him, a constant reminder of the commitments he could not escape. His attempts to sidestep his responsibilities did nothing to diminish the love and care his children received in his absence. They were growing up surrounded by support and love, finding strength in the lessons learned from their father's choices.

The story of their lives, though shaped by his absence, was not defined by it. Instead, it was marked by resilience and the unwavering belief that every child deserves a future filled with hope and opportunity. Despite the difficulties, they were learning to navigate life with strength and grace, embodying the values of love, respect, and perseverance.

In the end, the legacy of his choices was one of self- inflicted isolation and regret, while the lives of his children continued to flourish in a world built on love and integrity. The contrast was stark, but it underscored a powerful truth: that the absence of one can sometimes be the catalyst for a brighter and more fulfilling future for those left behind.

CHAPTER 11

In Sky's journey toward healing, she found solace and strength in her faith, embracing God as her sanctuary. She journeyed deeper into the abyss of her past, uncovering hidden emotions and unraveling the knots of pain. The scars on her heart, once raw and agonizing, began to fade as she found her voice and her strength. Through her transformation, she became an inspiration to those who felt their histories. Her children watched as their mother evolved, the profound lesson that the past didn't have to dictate the future.

CHAPTER 12

The man still ensnared in his self-made prison, faced a pivotal moment of reckoning. He could no longer evade the torment of his past, the pain he had caused, and the remorse that weighed on his conscience. He had arrived at a crossroads, where redemption beckoned. And he could no longer postpone the journey. As he grappled with his demons and sought to make amends, his isolation deepened. He began to question the choices he had made and the love he had forsaken. It was a journey towards understanding his own scars; seeking forgiveness, and rediscovering the light he had known.

CHAPTER 13

"Torn but Unbroken" transcended the confines of individual stories. It had evolved into a tapestry of collective healing, an anthem of resilience sung by many voices. It was no longer solely Sky's story; it was an amalgamation of experiences, a chorus of those who had tasted pain and triumph. Together, they faced their traumas, celebrated their victories, and continued to rebuild their lives. The woman, once broken, had become a pillar of strength for herself and countless others who found solace in her narrative.

CHAPTER 14

As she navigated the path of healing, she took refuge in the pages of her journal. Through her writing, she chronicled her transformation, recorded her progress, and shared the invaluable lessons she had learned. Her aspiration to publish her story was not one of a victim but a testament to the enduring human spirit. The writing process became a catharsis through which she could reflect on her past, her personal growth, and her dreams for the future. Through her words, she aimed to inspire, uplift, and ignite the spark of resilience in those who felt trapped by their circumstances.

CHAPTER 15

In parallel, the man had reached the precipice of his revelation. Faced with the consequences of his actions, he could no longer evade the torment he had caused. The weight of guilt served as a relentless reminder of the love he had spurned, and he longed for the opportunity to rebuild his life. Despite his solitary journey, he sought to confront his past, understand his scars, and pave a path toward redemption. It was an arduous path, but one he could no longer deny.

CHAPTER 16

At its core, "Torn but Unbroken" had transformed into a story of collective healing, reconciliation, and redemption. The narrative was no longer just about Sky's journey; it was about the broader spectrum of healing and growth she inspired. Through her resilience, she embodied the human capacity to heal, forgive, and rewrite the narrative of her life. Their story stood as a testament to the enduring resilience of the human spirit. Even the most broken among us can find their way back to wholeness. The story of "Torn but Unbroken" is a tribute to the indomitable spirit of those who refuse to be defined by the trials of their past. It's a narrative transformation, of turning pain into power and finding a new beginning in the wake of devastation. Above all, it's a testament to the enduring human capacity to heal, love, and thrive despite the hardest of circumstances.

CHAPTER 17

The world, with all its complexities, offered our protagonist a fresh canvas upon which to paint the story of her resurgence. As she ventured deeper into the realm to healing, her outreach to those who had endured similar hardships expanded. Her unwavering determination to break free from the past and construct a brighter future made her a beacon of hope to others. She dedicated herself to making a difference, advocating and sharing her experiences with those on the path to recovery. In their shared pain and triumph, they discovered the power of collective healing.

CHAPTER 18

Meanwhile, the man who had inflicted so much pain upon her remained mired in the consequences of his actions. Guilt, like an unshakable specter, haunted his every step. The life he had chosen was crumbling, and the solitude he had sought now seemed more desolate than ever.

CHAPTER 19

Strong In her quest for healing, the woman found solace in creative expression. She immersed herself in writing, art, and other outlets that allowed her to process her emotions and capture her journey. Through each piece she created, she explored the depths of her past, transforming pain into powerful narratives of hope and resilience. As she poured her heart into her work, she discovered a renewed sense of purpose and strength. Her creativity not only helped her heal but also served as a source of inspiration for others facing similar struggles. Her children watched as their mother channeled her experiences into something beautiful, learning that resilience and growth come from embracing one's own story and crafting a future defined by possibility.

CHAPTER 20

As time passed, Rabbit remained isolated, struggling with the relentless consequences of his actions. He found himself increasingly at odds with the world around him, his relationships fractured, and his opportunities dwindling. The life he once sought to escape had become a harsh reality, a stark reminder of the choices he had made.

He wandered through a life devoid of meaningful connections, where the echoes of his past decisions followed him relentlessly. His attempts to make amends often fell short, leaving him in a constant state of regret and frustration. The freedom he had once yearned for became a heavy burden, and he was forced to confront the reality that some wounds were too deep to heal.

As he faced the mounting challenges, it became clear that his journey was less about seeking redemption and more about enduring the fallout of his own making. His life, marked by missed opportunities and fractured relation- ships, stood as a testament to the cost of living a life disconnected from responsibility and genuine remorse.

Seeking forgiveness, and rediscovering the light he had once known.

CHAPTER 21

As the chapters of her life continued to unfold, the impact of Sky's journey began to resonate far beyond her immediate circle. The lessons learned and the strength she had cultivated became a beacon of hope for others facing their struggles. Her story, once a personal battle, evolved into a source of inspiration for those navigating tumultuous paths.

Sky's experiences sparked conversations about healing and growth, creating a ripple effect of empowerment that touched many lives. As she engaged in dialogues and shared her narrative, she found that her tale was not just one of survival but a guide for others seeking to reclaim their lives from adversity.

In her role as an advocate, Sky became a mentor, using her experiences to illuminate the way for both men and women grappling with similar challenges. Her legacy was not only in the personal victories she achieved but in the collective strength she helped nurture. The woman who had once been broken became a symbol of hope and transformation, proving that even in despair, one could rise to become a guiding force for others.

CHAPTER 22

As Sky continued her journey of healing, she found solace and strength in the simple, everyday moments that often went unnoticed. In her pursuit of recovery, she started embracing small joys and cultivating gratitude for the present. She began to appreciate the beauty of a sunrise, the laughter of her children, and the tranquility of quiet moments. Each day, she focused on the positive aspects of her life, finding peace in the routine and comfort in the familiar.

This newfound appreciation for the ordinary allowed Sky to rebuild her life on a foundation of mindfulness and presence. By cherishing these small moments, she discovered a renewed sense of purpose and connection. Her days became a tapestry of meaningful experiences, woven together by gratitude and love. Through this lens of appreciation, she learned to navigate her challenges with a lighter heart, using the lessons of her journey to inspire others to find beauty and strength in their own lives.

Sky's story transformed into one of embracing the present and finding joy in the everyday. Her ability to see the extraordinary in the ordinary became a beacon of hope for those seeking to rediscover the beauty in their own lives amidst their struggles.

CHAPTER 23

As Sky continued to heal, she found herself drawn to the power of forgiveness-not only toward others but also toward herself. She began to understand that true healing required letting go of lingering resentment and embracing forgiveness as a way to free herself from the chains of the past. This journey was deeply personal and transformative, as she learned to forgive not just those who had wronged her but also herself for the choices she had made along the way.

Sky's exploration of forgiveness became a central theme in her path to inner peace. She engaged in reflective practices, seeking to release the weight of past grievances and make space for compassion and understanding. Through this process, she discovered that forgiveness was not about forgetting or condoning the wrongs done to her but about finding the strength to move forward with grace.

Her journey toward forgiveness inspired those around her, demonstrating that letting go of bitterness could lead to a more profound sense of freedom and renewal. Sky's newfound perspective on forgiveness became a source of strength for others grappling with their struggles, showing them that it was possible to break free from the past and embrace a future filled with hope and possibility.

EMBRACING NEW
BEGINNINGS

As Sky's journey unfolded, she began to focus on creating a new life for herself and her children.

She realized that her past, while a significant part of her story, did not define her future. With this realization, she embraced the idea of new beginnings-a chapter in her life where she was the author of her destiny.

Sky started to explore her passions and dreams that had been put on hold. She enrolled in classes that piqued her interest, sought out new hobbies, and immersed herself in activities that brought her joy. This was her time to rediscover who she was outside the shadow of her past relationship. Her courage to step into the unknown became a beacon of hope for others, demonstrating that it was never too late to start over and pursue one's dreams.

Sky also began to teach her children the importance of resilience and the power of choice. She wanted them to understand that life's challenges could be stepping stones to something greater if faced with courage and determination. Her home became a place of love, learning, and growth-a sanctuary where her children could thrive.

Her story, now one of renewal and self-discovery, inspired those who felt trapped by their circumstances. Sky showed that healing wasn't just about mending what was broken but about building something new and beautiful from the pieces. She embodied the strength it takes to move forward, not with a focus on the past, but with a heart full of hope for the future.

A LEGACY OF STRENGTH

Sky's journey had come full circle, and as she reflected on her path, she saw not just the struggles but the immense growth she had undergone. Her life had become a testament to the power of resilience and the ability to rise above adversity. The legacy she was creating wasn't just about survival-it was about thriving in the face of hardship and building a purposeful future.

Sky understood that her story was one of many, yet it carried a unique power to inspire. She began to see herself as a role model, not just for her children but for anyone facing their battles. Her experiences had given her wisdom, and she felt a deep responsibility to share that wisdom with others. Through mentoring, speaking engagements, and writing, Sky began to extend her influence, helping others to find their paths to healing.

The legacy she left behind was one of strength, compassion, and unwavering determination. She had transformed her pain into a powerful force for good, proving that even in the darkest times, there was a way to find light. Sky's story was now a guiding light for others, showing them that no matter how broken one might feel, there was always a way to rebuild, rise, and create a life filled with meaning and joy.

CHAPTER 26

Amid the backdrop of Sky's individual and (A/ intertwined journeys, "Torn but Unbroken" began to touch the lives of people around the world. Readers from diverse backgrounds found solace and inspiration within the pages of Sky's stories. Readers who had once felt trapped in the shadows of their pasts now saw a glimmer of hope. They recognized that healing, transformation, and the capacity to rewrite one's narrative were not abstract concepts but attainable realities. The possibility of emerging from the darkest corners of one's life and finding the strength to rebuild became an indomitable truth.

CHAPTER 27

The pages of "Torn but Unbroken" bore witness to Sky's remarkable journey. This was not a tale shared with another; it was Sky's life, her pain, and her triumph. As the sole author, Sky poured her heart into every chapter, transforming her personal experiences into a powerful guide for others facing similar struggles. Her story was a beacon of hope, teaching and inspiring both men and women who had faced abuse and adversity. Through her words, Sky showed that no matter how broken one might feel, there is always a path to healing and strength. This was her legacy-a testament to resilience and the unwavering spirit that refuses to be shattered.

CHAPTER 28

The book's message was clear: no matter how torn and shattered life may become, there is always the potential for healing, growth, and the rekindling of a life worth living. Each page was a testament to the power of human resilience and the unwavering spirit of those who refused to be defined by the trials of their past.

CHAPTER 29

The closing chapter of "Torn but Unbroken" was not an ending but a new beginning. The woman, the man, and all those who had shared in their journey had learned that healing was an ongoing process, a lifelong commitment to rewriting their stories. Their lives were a testament to the human capacity to endure, transform, and emerge from the darkest of trials as stronger, more compassionate individuals. And so, the story continued, not as a tale of victimhood but as a testament to the triumph of the human spirit. It echoed the words of the poet Rumi, who said, "The wound is the place where the Light enters you." In their wounds, the light of resilience, redemption, and love had entered, illuminating a path forward to a brighter, unbroken tomorrow. Readers who had once felt trapped in the shadows of their pasts now saw a glimmer of hope. They recognized that healing, transformation, and the capacity to rewrite one's narrative were not abstract concepts but attainable realities. The possibility of emerging from the darkest corners of one's life and finding the strength to rebuild became a tangible promise. This narrative, full of pain and perseverance, celebrated the unbreakable spirit of those who refuse to be defined by their past. It was a powerful reminder that no matter how torn we may be, there is always hope for a brighter, unbroken future. The story continued, not as a tale of victimhood but as a testament to the triumph of the human spirit.

THE ENVY OF JEZEBEL

Jezebel's life was marked by a deep-seated naivety, clashing with a desperate hope that the man she loved, Rabbit, would one day reciprocate her affections. Little did she know, Rabbit had long deemed her unworthy, secretly labeling her as "trash" in the recesses of his heart. Despite her yearning and the pain of unrequited love, Jezebel was blind to the reality that Rabbit never saw her as someone worthy of respect or genuine affection.

Her envy toward Sky was palpable. Jezebel, driven by a desire to replicate Sky's success and attain the life she had built, spent years observing and attempting to mimic every aspect of Sky's existence. Yet, no matter how hard she tried, she remained ensnared in her past-a life marked by poverty and nothingness. Her attempts to elevate herself to Sky's level were in vain, a reflection of her inability to escape the limitations of her own choices and circumstances.

Sky's beauty and grace stood in stark contrast to Jezebel's appearance. Where Sky radiated warmth and elegance, Jezebel's lack of charm and disheveled appearance only served to amplify her envy and resentment. The contrast between them was not just physical but symbolic of their differing lives and values.

Jezebel's fixation on Sky and her relentless efforts to mirror her life only underscored her failures and the disparity between them. Her envy was not just a personal struggle but a broader reflection of her discontent and dissatisfaction with her own life. She remained entrenched in the shadows of Sky's achievements, unable to rise above her inadequacies.

Despite Rabbit and Jezebel's attempts to safeguard their secrets, believing they would remain forever concealed, history has shown that hidden truths have a way of surfacing. As Sky continues her journey of healing and empowerment, Jezebel's attempts to sabotage or replicate her life are ultimately futile. The divine intervention that unveils hidden truths serves as a reminder that true transformation and success come from within, and no amount of envy or deceit can change that reality.

THE POWER OF EFFECTIVE COMMUNICATION

As Sky's journey draws to a close, the importance of effective communication becomes a central theme. In every relationship, communication serves as the bridge that connects hearts and minds. This chapter delves into the art of communicating clearly and compas-sionately, offering practical tools for fostering under- standing and resolution.

Effective communication begins with active listening- truly hearing and validating the other person's perspective. It's about more than just exchanging words; it's about creating a space where both parties feel heard and respected. Sky's story highlights how this practice can transform conflicts into opportunities for growth and connection.

Key principles of effective communication include:

- **Speak with clarity and honesty:** Share your thoughts and feelings openly, without ambiguity. Being direct yet respectful helps avoid misunderstandings and builds trust.
- **Practice active listening:** Focus fully on what the other person is saying. Reflect on what you hear to ensure understanding, and ask clarifying questions if needed.

- **Stay calm and composed:** Approach conversations with a calm demeanor, even during disagreements. Managing your emotions helps keep the dialogue constructive and respectful.
- **Use "I" statements:** Express your feelings and needs using "I" statements rather than "you" statements. This reduces defensiveness and focuses on your own experience, e.g., "I feel upset when..." rather than "Yiou a1ways...".
- **Seek Common Ground:** Aim to find mutual understanding and solutions that benefit both parties. Collaborate on finding compromises and solutions rather than focusing on what went wrong.
- **Be open to feedback:** Embrace constructive criticism as an opportunity for growth. Approach feedback with an open mind and a willingness to adapt.
- **Set Boundaries Respectfully:** Communicate your boundaries and needs. Respecting each other's limits fosters a healthier and more supportive relationship.

Sky's experiences demonstrate that effective communication not only resolves conflicts but also strengthens relationships. As she reflects on her journey, she recognizes that mastering these skills is essential for moving forward, whether in closing one chapter or opening another.

ENCOURAGEMENT FOR THE
PATH AHEAD

As you navigate the end of a relationship or any challenging situation, remember that effective communication is key to both resolution and growth. It's a skill that can enhance your interactions and relation- ships, fostering a deeper understanding and connection with others.

In embracing effective communication, you empower yourself to face future challenges with confidence. The journey of self-discovery and healing continues beyond the end of a relationship, offering new opportunities for personal growth and meaningful connections.

Sky's story is a testament to the resilience of the human spirit and the transformative power of clear, compassionate communication. As you move forward, take with you the lessons of effective dialogue, and let them guide you toward a future filled with hope, understanding, and fulfilling relationships.

UNDERSTANDING HEALTHY RELATIONSHIPS

A healthy relationship is built on mutual respect, trust, and communication. It's essential to recognize the foundations of a positive partnership:

- **Mutual Respect:** Respect each other's opinions, boundaries, and individuality. This means valuing each other's thoughts and feelings and acknowledging each other's worth.
- **Trust and Honesty:** Trust is a cornerstone of any relationship. Honesty fosters trust, and trust builds a strong, reliable bond. Open and truthful communication helps maintain this trust.
- **Effective Communication:** Clear and open communication is crucial. It involves actively listening to each other, expressing needs and feelings honestly, and addressing conflicts calmly and constructively.
- **Support and Encouragement:** A healthy relationship involves supporting each other's goals and aspirations. Encouragement and constructive feedback strengthen the partnership and individual growth.
- **Equality and Shared Responsibility:** Both partners should share responsibilities and decisions. Equality in a relationship

means that both individuals have a voice and contribute to the relationship's success.

IDENTIFYING SIGNS OF AN UNHEALTHY RELATIONSHIP

It's important to recognize the signs of an unhealthy relationship to address issues before they escalate.

- **Control and manipulation:** One partner may attempt to control or manipulate the other, undermining their autonomy and decision- making.
- **Constant Criticism:** Excessive or harsh criticism can erode self-esteem and create a toxic environment.
- **Isolation:** An unhealthy partner may try to isolate the other from friends and family, limiting their support network.
- **Unresolved Conflict:** Persistent arguments and conflicts that are not addressed constructively can lead to long-term dissatisfaction and harm.
- **Abuse:** Any form of abuse-whether physical, emotional, psychological, or verbal-is a serious red flag. Abuse is never acceptable and should never be tolerated.

RECOGNIZING AND RESPONDING TO ABUSE

"Abuse in any form 1s unacceptable and must be addressed promptly."

- **Types of Abuse:** Abuse can be physical (e.g., hitting, pushing), emotional (e.g., belittling, threatening), psychological (e.g., manipulating, controlling), or verbal (e.g., insults, threats).
- **Immediate Response:** If you or someone you know is experiencing abuse, seek help immediately. This may include contacting a trusted friend, family member, or professional.
- **Creating a Safety Plan:** Develop a safety plan to ensure personal safety. This includes identifying a safe place to go, having important documents ready, and knowing how to contact emergency services.
- **Seeking Professional Help:** Reach out to counselors, therapists, or domestic violence support organizations for assistance and resources.
- **Reporting Abuse:** Report abuse to the appropriate authorities. This may involve contacting law enforcement or filing a report with a local domestic violence agency.

SUPPORT SYSTEMS AND RESOURCES

Building a support system is crucial for overcoming abuse and maintaining healthy relationships.

- **Local Support Organizations:** Connect with local organizations that offer support for abuse victims. These organizations provide resources, counseling, and legal assistance.

- **Hotlines and Helplines:** Utilize hotlines and helplines for immediate support and guidance. These services offer confidential assistance and can help you navigate the next steps.

- **Counseling and Therapy:** Professional counseling can provide emotional support and strategies for healing. Therapy can help individuals process their experiences and rebuild their lives.

- **Support Groups:** Join support groups where individuals with similar experiences can offer advice, share their stories, and provide mutual encouragement.

- **Legal Assistance:** Seek legal advice to understand your rights and options. Legal professionals can assist with restraining orders, custody issues, and other legal matters related to abuse.

EMPOWERING YOURSELF AND OTHERS

"Empowerment is key to breaking free from abusive situations and fostering healthy relationships."

- **Building Self-Esteem:** Focus on building self- esteem and self-worth. Recognize your value and understand that you deserve respect and kindness.
- **Setting Boundaries:** Establish and communicate clear boundaries in relationships. Boundaries help maintain personal space and prevent unhealthy behaviors.
- **Educating Yourself:** Learn about healthy relationships, abuse dynamics, and coping strategies. Knowledge equips you to make informed decisions and seek appropriate help.
- **Supporting Others:** Offer support and encouragement to those in difficult situations.

Being a supportive friend or family member can make a significant difference in someone's life.

- **Promoting Awareness:** Advocate for awareness and education on relationship health and abuse prevention. Raising awareness helps create a more informed and supportive community.

NAVIGATING THE END OF A RELATIONSHIP

Ending a relationship, especially one involving abuse, can be challenging. Here's how to approach it with care and clarity:

- **Making the Decision:** Reflect on the reasons for ending the relationship and ensure that it is the right choice for your well-being and safety.
- **Communicating Clearly:** When ending a relationship, communicate your decision clearly and calmly. Avoid blame or confrontation, and focus on your own needs and feelings.
- **Planning for Transition:** Prepare for the transition by making practical arrangements, such as finding a new place to live or managing shared responsibilities.
- **Prioritizing Self-Care:** Take care of yourself emotionally and physically during this time.

Engage in activities that promote well-being and seek support from loved ones.

- **"Moving Forward:** Embrace the opportunity for a fresh start. Focus on personal growth and building healthy relationships in the future."

NO EXCUSE FOR ABUSE

There is no justification for any form of abuse. Abuse is harmful, and unacceptable, and should never be tolerated.

- **Understanding Abuse:** Recognize that abuse is about power and control, not about the victim's behavior or actions. No one deserves to be abused.
- **Addressing Myths:** Dispel common myths about abuse, such as blaming the victim or believing that abuse is a private matter. Abuse is a serious issue that requires intervention and support.
- **Seeking Justice:** Hold abusers accountable for their actions. Seek justice through legal channels and support services.
- **Encouraging Help-Seeking:** Encourage those affected by abuse to seek help and support.

Empower them to take action and access the resources they need.

- **Building a Supportive Community:** Foster a community that supports victims of abuse and works toward prevention. Promote education and awareness to combat abuse and support healthy relationships.

INTRODUCTION AND PURPOSE

It is my heartfelt prayer that God guides you on your journey in your relationships. Relationships can be profoundly fulfilling, but they must be built on the right foundation. Too often, people find themselves in relationships for the wrong reasons or out of selfish- ness. It's crucial to recognize when a relationship is not serving your well-being and to let go rather than hold on for personal gain. This message aims to encourage you to live in happiness and peace, to be with someone who loves you genuinely, and to understand that God is love. By breaking the cycle of games and fostering real support, we can build relationships based on mutual respect and genuine affection.

RECOGNIZING THE RIGHT REASONS FOR BEING TOGETHER

Many relationships are formed based on superficial reasons or personal convenience. It's important to reflect on why you are with someone:

- **Authentic Connection:** Ensure that your relationship is based on a genuine connection rather than superficial qualities or convenience. True love stems from mutual respect, shared values, and deep emotional bonds.

- **Self-awareness:** Understand your motivations for being in a relationship. Are you with this person because you genuinely care for them, or are you seeking validation, security, or other personal gains?

- **Compatibility and Growth:** Assess whether the relationship allows both partners to grow and thrive. A healthy relationship should support personal development and encourage both individuals to pursue their goals and dreams.

- **Respect and Equality:** Relationships should be based on equality and respect, not power dynamics or control. Both partners should feel valued and heard.

THE IMPORTANCE OF LETTING GO

Sometimes, letting go is the best decision for both individuals involved. Here's why it's important:

- **Honoring Your Feelings:** If you realize that the relationship is not fulfilling or healthy, it's important to honor your feelings and recognize when it's time to move on. Staying in a relationship for the wrong reasons can cause more harm than good.

- **Avoiding Selfish Motives:** Don't hold on to a relationship for personal gain or out of a sense of obligation. It's important to be honest with yourself and your partner about your feelings and intentions.

- **Respect for Both Parties:** Letting go respectfully allows both individuals to find the right paths for their lives. It's a way to show respect for each other's future and personal growth.

- **"Healing and Moving Forward:** Ending a relationship can be challenging, but it also provides an opportunity for healing and growth. Use this time to reflect, heal, and prepare for healthier relationships in the future."

"BREAKING FREE FROM EXCUSES"

Many people make excuses for staying in unhealthy relationships. It's essential to break free from these justifications.

- **No Justification for Unhappiness:** There is no valid reason to remain in a relationship that causes unhappiness or harm. A relationship should bring joy and fulfillment, not stress and distress.

- **Addressing Common Excuses:** Recognize and challenge common excuses for staying in unhealthy relationships, such as the fear of being alone, societal expectations, or a belief that things will improve on their own.

- **Prioritizing Well-Being:** Your mental, emotional, and physical well-being should be a priority. Do not compromise your health or happiness for the sake of maintaining a relationship.

- **Empowerment and Choice:** Empower yourself to make choices that align with your values and needs. Remember that you have the right to pursue a relationship that genuinely contributes to your happiness.

EMBRACING TRUE LOVE AND PEACE

Finding and nurturing true love involves being with someone who reciprocates your feelings and treats you with respect.

- **Genuine Love:** True love is characterized by mutual affection, support, and understanding. It is not about possessing someone or fulfilling personal needs but about sharing a meaningful connection.
- **Living in Peace:** Peace in a relationship comes from knowing that both partners are committed to each other's well-being. It involves creating a harmonious environment where both individuals can thrive.
- **Mutual Support:** A healthy relationship involves supporting each other's dreams and challenges.

True partners stand by each other through difficulties and celebrate each other's successes.

- **God's Love:** Embrace the concept that "God is love." By aligning your relationship with the principles of divine love, you foster a bond that is nurturing, respectful, and enduring.

UNDERSTANDING THE ROLE OF REAL MEN AND WOMEN

Healthy relationships require both partners to fulfill their roles authentically and with integrity.

- **Real Men:** A real man supports and provides for his partner, not just financially but also emotionally and spiritually. He is a source of strength, compassion, and reliability.
- **Real Women:** A real woman stands by her partner, supporting him in his endeavors and being a source of encouragement and love. She values partnership and mutual respect.
- **Equality and respect:** Both partners should contribute to the relationship with respect and equality. There should be a balance of giving and receiving, where both individuals are valued.
- **Commitment and Integrity:** Both men and women should demonstrate commitment and integrity in their relationships. This involves being honest, reliable, and dedicated to each other's well-being.

"BREAKING THE CYCLE OF GAMES"

Relationships built on games and manipulation are harmful and unproductive. Here's how to foster genuine connections:

- **Avoiding Manipulation:** Avoid using manipulation or control tactics in relationships. Instead, focus on honest and direct communication to address issues and resolve conflicts.
- **Fostering Transparency:** Be transparent with your feelings, intentions, and expectations. Clear communication reduces misunderstandings and fosters trust.
- **Building Trust:** Trust is fundamental to any healthy relationship. Build and maintain trust through consistent actions, honesty, and reliability.
- **Encouraging Openness:** Encourage open and respectful discussions about relationship dynamics. Address issues directly rather than using passive-aggressive behavior or hidden agendas.

LIVING A LIFE OF LOVE AND FULFILLMENT

Ultimately, your journey in relationships should lead to a life of love, fulfillment, and happiness.

- **Choosing Happiness:** Prioritize your happiness and well-being. Seek relationships that enhance your life and align with your values and desires.
- **Pursuing Personal Growth:** Use your relationship experiences as opportunities for personal growth. Learn from your experiences and apply these lessons to future relationships.
- **Embracing True Connection:** Strive for connections that are authentic and fulfilling. True relationships are characterized by mutual respect, love, and support.
- **Reflecting Divine Love:** Reflect the love and principles of God in your relationships. By embodying divine love, you create a positive, nurturing environment for yourself and your partner.
- **Living Fully:** Embrace life fully by making choices that lead to personal and relational fulfillment. Celebrate the joys and face challenges with a spirit of resilience and hope.

www.ingramcontent.com/pod-product-compliance
Lightning Source LLC
Chambersburg PA
CBHW040914010826
48978CB00013BB/1281